IF I HAD A ROBOT

dan yaccarino

PUFFIN BOOKS

PUFFIN BOOKS   Published by the Penguin Group
Penguin Putnam Inc., 375 Hudson Street, New York, New York 10014, U.S.A.
Penguin Books Ltd, 27 Wrights Lane, London W8 5TZ, England
Penguin Books Australia Ltd, Ringwood, Victoria, Australia
Penguin Books Canada Ltd, 10 Alcorn Avenue, Toronto, Ontario, Canada M4V 3B2
Penguin Books (N.Z.) Ltd, 182-190 Wairau Road, Auckland 10, New Zealand

Penguin Books Ltd, Registered Offices: Harmondsworth, Middlesex, England

First published in the United States of America by Viking, a division of Penguin Books USA Inc., 1996
Published by Puffin Books, a member of Penguin Putnam Books for Young Readers, 1998

1 3 5 7 9 10 8 6 4 2

THE LIBRARY OF CONGRESS HAS CATALOGED THE VIKING EDITION AS FOLLOWS:
Yaccarino, Dan. If I had a robot / by Dan Yaccarino. p. cm.
Summary: Phil imagines the advantages of having a robot, from
feeding it his vegetables to becoming king of the playground.
ISBN 0-670-86936-8 [1. Robots—Fiction. 2. Behavior—Fiction.]
I. Title.
PZ7.Y125If 1996 [E]—dc20 95-26444 CIP AC

Puffin Books ISBN 0-14-056294-X

Printed in Singapore

SPECIAL THANKS TO THE ROBOT FROM "LOST IN SPACE," TOBOR, ROBBIE THE ROBOT, GIGANTOR, THE ROCK 'EM SOCK 'EM ROBOTS AND EVERY SPECIAL MECHANICAL PAL NOT MENTIONED HERE.

"Phil," Mom said, "you can't leave the dinner table until you finish your vegetables."

Boy!
I hate
vegetables!
I wish
someone
else would
eat them
for me!

I bet if I had a robot he would eat those vegetables at my command!

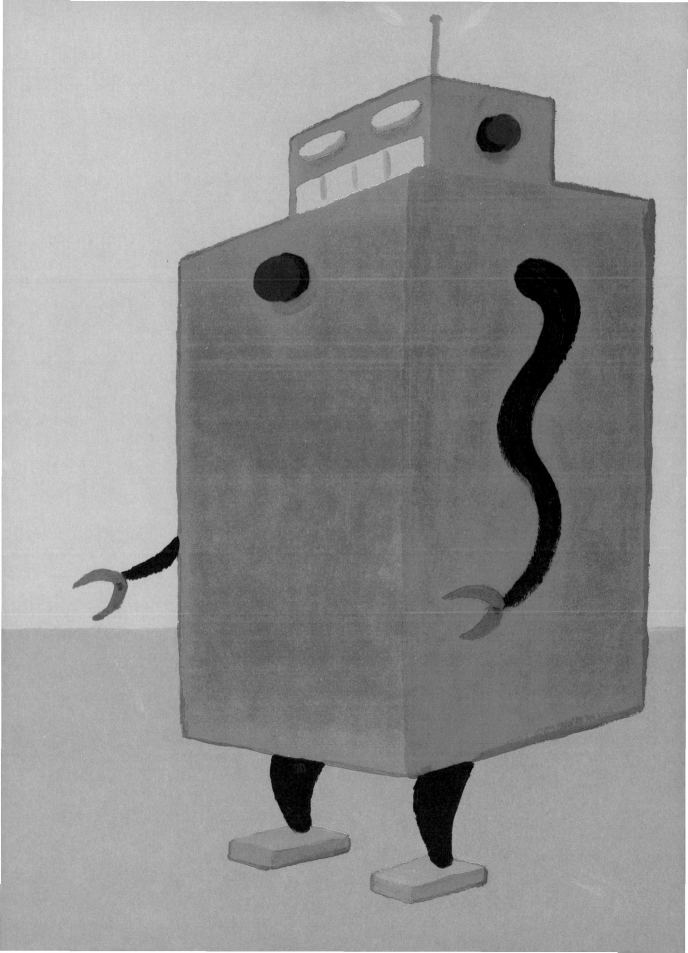

Yessiree!
With just
the flick
of a switch,
he'd eat
all my
lima
beans,
cauli-
flower,
and
brussels
sprouts.
Yuck!

And piano lessons, too!

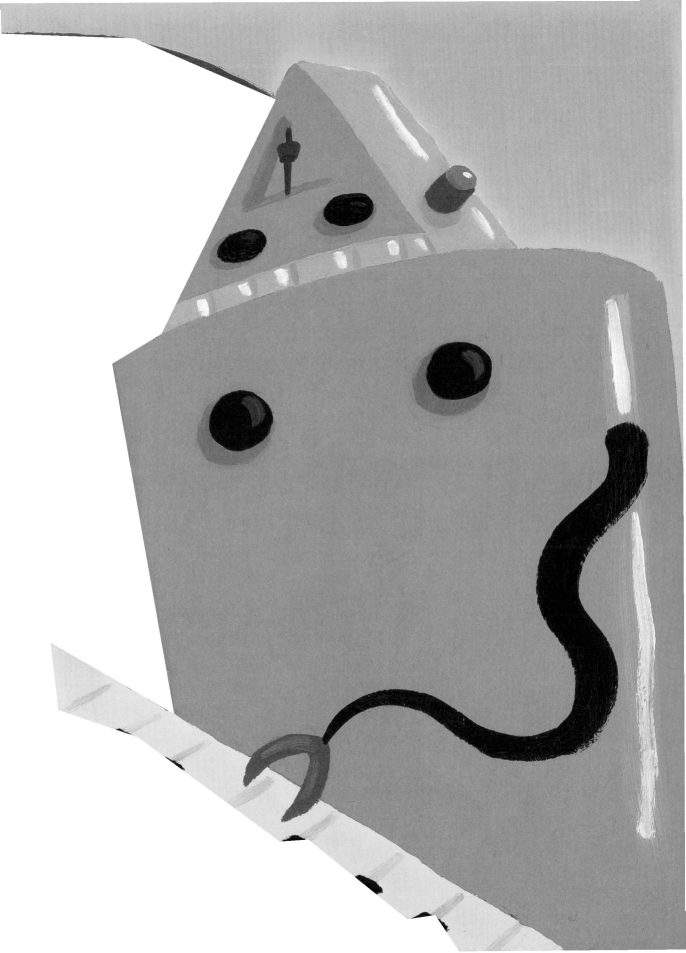

Boy! He could do everything

I don't want to do!

Why, he could even kiss my Aunt Louise!

And go to school so I don't have to!

No hotshot could ever hit a home run when we're in left field.

And those kids wouldn't dare pick on me if I had a robot. Gee, I'd be king of the play-ground!

Hey! With my robot
I could be king
of the whole world!

Wait! I could be master of the entire universe! And—

"Oh Phil . . ." my mom called. "Whoever eats their vegetables gets chocolate cake for dessert!"

Like I always say, if you want something done right, you've got to do it yourself!